Syrena's Curse

The Keeper Of The Light, Volume 1

Kristen Cole

Published by Kristen Cole, 2024.

While every precaution has been taken in the preparation of this book, the publisher assumes no responsibility for errors or omissions, or for damages resulting from the use of the information contained herein.

SYRENA'S CURSE

First edition. July 14, 2024.

ISBN: 979-8227046260

Written by Kristen Cole.

Table of Contents

"In loving memory of my uncles, who now live among the stars, and always reminded me that words have the power to change the world."

Chapter 1

"Hey! Who are you?"

Her father's voice snapped Syrena Davis out of her thoughts, and she looked over at him to see what he was talking about. His salt and pepper hair was disheveled more of late, and his graying beard had grown out and was unkempt. The worry lines in his forehead and around his eyes were easily seen. But it was the look in his eyes that scared her.

He was looking ahead, into the lush gardens that took up nearly the entirety of the back of their grand manor. The same gardens her mother had loved to spend her days in for so long. Following his sights, she saw a person standing at the edge of the garden. Syrena hadn't seen her there when they entered; how was she there now?

When the person turned, Syrena heard her father gasp. Syrena did the same. She was the most beautiful woman Syrena had ever seen. Even from the distance she could see the woman's blonde hair that seemed to be shimmering where the sun touched it. Round brown eyes and angelic features locked onto her father, and a golden dress that matched her hair completed the woman's beautiful brilliance. Syrena had never seen a woman so enchanting.

But then again, she hadn't ventured out of the manor in so long.

A warm breeze seemed to pick up out of nowhere, hitting Syrena's face and making her feel happy. Her father, though, didn't share in the glory.

"No..." he whispered to himself. "Not you...no..."

"Jonas." The woman's voice was heavenly and warm and devoid of the Irish accent Syrena and her father had. It was closer to British, but not quite.

The woman looked at her father with pity and resolve in her eyes and sighed. The White Light is fading and the darkness is stirring." Where is Annabel?"

Her father seemed to get a hold of his shock and swallowed hard. His eyes went to the garden around them. "She's...gone."

The woman, conversely, didn't look shocked to hear the news at all. Her eyes fell to Syrena. "Then, is her daughter ready to take her responsibility?"

Syrena's brow bunched. "What responsibility?"

The woman seemed to lean back as a look of disbelief took over her features. Anger filled her expression as her eyes shot back up to Jonas. "You haven't told her?"

Jonas swallowed hard again and retreated a step. "I..."

"You know what's at stake, what the darkness will do, and you didn't prepare her? Jonas, do you realize what you have done?"

Her father dropped to his knees and bowed his head before the woman. Syrena watched in awe as he looked up at her and clasped his hands together. "Please, Luna. She's all I have left."

Luna, though, did not give any mercy. "And you risked *losing* that by keeping her in the dark. Do you realize what you've done, Jonas? Have you forgotten your vows? Has greed and darkness taken you?"

Jonas, now bowed down with his forehead to the ground, nodded in spite of himself. "I have lost my way. Please, I beg your forgiveness."

Luna watched the back of his head, then looked over at Syrena. Her features softened and a small smile touched her lips.

"My name is Luna," she said.

"I'm Syrena. Please." She stepped closer to her father and put a hand on his shoulder. "My father didn't mean it. We are just a normal family. Let us be."

A scowl touched Luna's perfect brow, and she looked down at the back of her father's head again.

"You haven't told her the truth about who she is?" Luna's voice was becoming louder. "You've let her believe she was a normal child all this time?!"

Her father seemed to shrink further into the ground under Syrena's hand, but he finally looked up. "I just wanted to protect her. She's...she's all I have."

"Protect me from *what*?" Syrena wanted to know.

"Regardless, she deserves to know the truth. It is her choice to wield the White Light, but she should have had that choice long ago. You've failed us, Jonas." Luna looked to Syrena again, and again her features softened. "Do you want to know who you are, child? Who your mother really was? What you are destined to do?"

Syrena looked down at her father, who met her eyes with tears in his. His throat bobbed and he nodded slightly.

Syrena looked back to Luna's expressionless face. "Yes."

"I'm sorry, Syrena."

"Why didn't you tell me?"

Jonas looked over at his daughter, who didn't look back as they walked ahead.

"It wasn't important," he said, trying to sound confident.

"I still have a right to know, Father!" She looked up at her father. "Why didn't you tell me I'm a princess? That my mom was a princess? That I have a greater purpose?"

Jonas studied his daughter. Thinking about Annabel even now brought a pain to his heart. The man sighed softly as he ran his fingers through his hair. He hated to admit it, but she had a point. She did have a right to know just who her mother was, who *she* was.

Jonas stopped her and looked her in the eyes. "I thought that you...you'd been through enough. It's my job to protect you. Annabel just passed. I...I wanted to give us time to heal."

That was a lie. He knew that Annabel's magic would fall to his daughter, but he didn't want to face the repercussions of that. Not yet. For just a little while, he wanted to have a normal life with the only family he had left.

Before his time was up.

The way she searched his eyes reminded him so much of Annabel. She was so much like her mother it was painful to watch sometimes.

Strangely, she seemed to relax. The anger in her eyes dissipated, and a sympathy replaced it.

"I know this has been hard on you," she said, some of the fire leaving her voice. "You've...changed since Mother died. You're not as happy as you used to be, but I deserve to know *this*." Syrena's resolve returned. "And now, I have this curse."

Jonas' emotions overflowed. He dropped to his knees and wrapped his daughter in his arms. It was his fault! She never would have had to go through this if he had just been honest with her.

"I'm sorry, Syrena," he sobbed. "It's my fault. You're right. I should have told you everything."

He felt her hands on his back as he sobbed into her.

"It's okay, Father."

Sniffling, he leaned back and looked at her. She was smiling at him. A smile that looked just like her mother's.

"I'm sixteen," she continued. "We have five years to find the signs. There's plenty of time to break the curse."

That was just like Annabel. Finding some way to keep hope alive, even in the worst situations. It was one of the things that made him fall in love with Annabel so long ago.

He nodded, smiling through his tears. "You're right." He sniffled again and got a hold on his emotions. "We have time. I'm not sure what the signs are, but we can come up with a way to find them." He pulled her into another softer hug. "I promise, from now on I'll be different. I'm going to do everything I can to help you break this curse. Even if it's the last thing I do."

His breath caught in his throat. He didn't mean to say that. But Syrena didn't seem to catch what he meant. She nodded against him and broke the hug, sitting down on a nearby bench. The same bench she and Annabel used to share as they looked out at their favorite roses. When he'd once asked why, she told him it was the place she felt closest to her now that she was gone.

He watched as Syrena looked out at the roses again, but by the look in her eyes he could tell she wasn't really seeing them. He plucked one of the fine roses and suddenly understood why Syrena sat on the bench. Just holding a rose made him feel Annabel's spirit nearby. An anger filled him. It wasn't fair. To him. To her. He gulped hard with the realization that he had caused so much damage.

After informing Syrena of her responsibility now that Annabel was gone, Luna told them that Syrena would have a barrier to fulfilling her destiny. "Barrier" was putting it mildly.

It was a curse. Luna's...test for Syrena. And it was *his* fault. Had it not been for him, the curse never would have befallen onto Syrena. He hated it, hated himself for what he'd done to his daughter. Now, he'd made it even harder for her. For everyone.

When she sniffled, he was jolted back into the present, and he realized he'd been squeezing the rose in his hand. The broken, crumpled pedals unfolded a bit as he opened his hand once more, and he breathed another sigh. Syrena was right about one thing: his anger was at a new level. Little things that never bothered him before seemed to send him over the edge.

Tears stung his eyes with the pressure put on Syrena. But he choked them down. He'd made a promise to his daughter. Now was not the time for tears. He would spend the rest of his days doing whatever he could to help his daughter overcome the impossible obstacles placed on her because of him. He could be better. He *would* be better.

For Syrena.

For Annabel.

For everyone.

And he would keep nothing else from her. Starting today.

He realized he needed to start. Might as well get the worst part over with. "Syrena, there's something else you should know."

"Hurry Miss Syrena! Your father wants to speak with you."

Syrena placed a hand on her chest. "Frankie, you frightened me."

"My apologies, Miss Syrena."

She looked over at him, the only member of the staff willing to step foot in the garden. It had been years since she had sat in there like this, getting lost in the grand floral arrangements. Years since the encounter with the woman in their garden. Years since she had learned she was royalty, that she had a greater purpose in the world. Her father had wanted to protect her, and back then she didn't realize how right he was.

Once word got out about Her Heiress Syrena, young men came from all over the world to try and win her heart. How word had gotten out was a mystery unto itself. Luna's doing, no doubt. She seemed content to test Syrena at every turn. The young men who visited were brazen, commenting openly on her midnight black hair and sapphire blue eyes, that she was "the most beautiful princess they'd ever seen", but she could tell their intentions weren't pure. Their ulterior motives were aplenty: access to her land, having a princess as a trophy wife, one even fancied himself a prince and wanted to "create a new world order together". Syrena began to think everyone outside the manor was evil. Maybe it was good that her father had practically kept her captive in the grand home unless she was accompanying him around town.

And then Frankie came.

Once her father's health began to deteriorate, Frankie appeared to help Syrena with her day-to-day life. He never said it, but she suspected her father had called for him to come help. Frankie wasn't a new face; they'd known each other since childhood. In a moment of vulnerability, Syrena even once thought Frankie was the one meant to win her heart.

He was an imposing figure, towering head and shoulders over her with broad shoulders and a thin, clean-shaven face. His prominent nose, thin lips, and square jaw were attractive. To say nothing about his emerald-green eyes. Perhaps the most attractive feature about him was his willingness to do anything in order to accomplish any goal he set out to accomplish. Including disobeying her father's direct orders. Since he was bedridden, her father forbade anyone else but Syrena from going into the garden. He made Frankie promise he'd never set foot in there. Yet here Frankie was, fetching Syrena to once again make sure things were done in a quick and orderly fashion. It wasn't like her father could get out of bed to physically stop him.

He was also aware of the potential suitors visiting, hoping to be chosen by Her Heiress. He truly hoped the best for her, and she could see it pained him to see her alone, though he never spoke of it.

And she never spoke of the man from her dreams, the one she truly waited on.

For several months now she'd dreamed of him. Of her sitting on the bench facing the sea and his tall, shadowed frame approaching her in a strange fog. She could feel his pure heart, even in the dream. A sort of warmth that blanketed her and made her feel safe. She could almost hear him whispering her name as he reached out to her, holding a rose that matched her favorites from the garden. She'd hold her hand out to him, but just as their fingers touched, she'd wake. She had some feeling that he was her true love. And that he was coming.

Today, a sadness she had never seen clouded Frankie's features. Something was wrong.

"How many times do I have to tell you that you don't have to call me that, Frankie," Syrena said. "You can call me Rena, like always."

"We're not children anymore, Miss. It's appropriate to address you as your royal title."

Syrena breathed a sigh. She knew arguing with Frankie was futile. "I'll be right up."

Frankie nodded. "Hurry," he quickly added before rushing back toward the house.

With a sigh, Syrena climbed to her feet and followed her friend's path. She spent most nights with her father. His condition was ever worsening. She knew their time together was coming to an end.

Syrena looked up into the clear night sky as she went, idly wondering if her mother was looking down on them. Looking at the mess her family had become. Inside the manor, Syrena ascended the carved, dark brown wooden stairs. Her father's room was on the first door on the left, and she took a deep breath as she reached it, preparing herself for what was to come.

She knocked lightly before she opened the door. "Father?" There was no answer, but she knew where to find him and continued fully into his room.

A single candle at his bedside offered dim light in the room, and she saw his head turn toward her. His eyes were sunken into his head and his cheeks that were so full of life were now devoid of it. He was looking more and more like a skeleton with each passing week.

"Rena." His voice came out like it took a great effort.

"Good evening, Father." She took his hand when he offered it. "How are you feeling today?"

Jonas gave her hand a gentle squeeze. "I'm afraid I don't...have much time left, Rena."

She patted his hand with her free one. "You say that every night, Father."

"I know." He gave hers another gentle squeeze. "There's something I want to...to say to you."

His stamina was dropping more and more. Nowadays, he could hardly give her a sentence without having to stop to breathe.

"What is it, Father?"

"I...I want you to know...that I'm s-...sorry."

"For what?" she wanted to know. She didn't like the sound of this.

"That I f-...failed you. That...you're being punished...for my choices."

Syrena stared down at the man in bed. He looked pale and...frail. The tears started coming sooner than usual, and she did her best to hide them. He'd declined so far, losing his hair and body weight. Memories of the man he used to be passed through her mind.

He'd held up his end of the promise he made to her and changed. Immediately he was the happy man she remembered from her childhood. He was friendly with the staff and smiled more than he had since her mother died. The manor was once again filled with joy and love and laughter. It was like the cancer he'd told her about never existed at all. They'd even taken day trips away from the manor, though they were careful to return before midnight. He'd become the man she loved so much.

But week by week, his energy declined. He would retire to bed earlier and earlier. At first she didn't mind it. "A product of getting older," he'd say with a laugh. But when he started losing weight, Syrena knew it was not just his age.

Since that day in the garden where Luna told Syrena about her destiny, he had completely changed. He'd once again become the man she remembered when her mother was alive. Happy, less bothered by trivial things.

Now, here he was, a shell of himself. And he was apologizing to her?

She scooted closer to him. "I don't blame you, Father," she reassured him. "You did what you thought was best."

He stared at her a moment, and then smiled and squeezed her hand again. "You're j-...just like your...mother. So...pure." He took a few deep breaths. "I never meant...to hurt you. I'm sorry that...I must leave."

The tears were flowing freely now. She sniffled. "I know, Father. You've been alone for so long. It's time for you to rejoin Mother. I have this manor and the staff and Frankie. I'll be alright."

He nodded as best he could. "You...you'll break...the curse, Rena. I know you will." He looked over at her. "Promise me you'll...never...give up."

They'd looked. They'd looked high and low for any sign, but in the last four years they didn't find a single clue as to where she could find one. Still, he'd kept her spirits high when she thought it was hopeless. What was she supposed to do now?

She brought their clasped hands up to her cheek as she nodded tearfully. "I promise. I'll never give up."

With her help, he moved the back of his hand against her full cheek and gave her the best smile he could. She looked into the eyes of the man she would miss so much. The first man to ever show her pure, unaltered love.

And she stayed with him, by his bedside, until he took his last breath.

"Lady Syrena?"

Syrena sniffled in surprise. "Yes?"

She heard the sound of her door open as the familiar voice spoke up again.

"It's Mrs. Scott, dear. The staff was wondering if it was okay for them to go. The chores are...oh, Lady Syrena."

Syrena buried her head into the pillow to try and hide her grief. The sobs seemed to take over her body. She couldn't stop them.

A hand on her back warmed her. "Oh, Lady Syrena, I'm so sorry about your father."

Syrena shook her head into the pillow. "I'm not ready for this. I'm not ready to be alone."

Mrs. Scott rubbed her back gently. "I wish there was something I could say to make this better."

A moan escaped her throat. "What am I going to do now? I haven't even found a sign yet."

The hand on her back froze. "A sign? A sign of what?"

Syrena froze herself. She hadn't meant to say that, but as she thought about it, what choice did she have?

With a sniffle, she turned from her pillow and looked at her family friend. The Scottish woman's graying blonde hair was short and lay flat on her head. Her blue eyes were a picture of sorrow and her thin lips were dropped in a sympathetic frown.

Syrena took a settling breath. "I'm cursed, Mrs. Scott. I have one year to break the curse or the entire town will be drowned in darkness."

Mrs. Scott tilted her head and blinked. "What do you mean?"

"It..." Syrena sighed again. "It happened a long time ago. I got a curse put on me...because of my father."

Chapter 2

"My mother was the keeper of an ancient magic that goes back further than I know," Syrena explained. "It's called the White Light. It protects the town from a dark magic that's trying to take over. My mother was supposed to prepare me to be the keeper, but she died before she could. My father decided not to tell me about it, so after Mother passed we were visited by an enchantress named Luna.

"Luna saw what my father had become and was afraid that I wasn't fit to be the keeper of the White Light, so she decided to test me. She put a curse on me that will be fulfilled on my twenty-first birthday. I have to find the signs and prove my purity before I turn twenty-one or the darkness will consume the town." Syrena hesitated. Even as she explained, she felt like a failure. "I don't know how many signs there are, what they are, or how to find them. My father and I tried for the last four years and we haven't found anything. I don't even know where they *could* be."

When she finished, she looked over at Mrs. Scott, who nodded and turned to the staff.

"With that said, if anyone would like to leave the manor, now is your chance to do so. No hard feelings, no questions asked."

Syrena looked at the staff, still dressed in their brown pants and white shirts. No one left.

"Good," Mrs. Scott continued, "on to the next point then. Any ideas on how we can find a sign?"

"Is the sign something living or, like...an object or something?" came a reply.

Syrena shrugged. "Luna didn't give me any information about that."

"Have you had any strange dreams?"

Syrena opened her mouth to deny the comment, and then she quickly looked over at Mrs. Scott. "Actually, I *have* had a dream about a man with a yellow rose. I have had it almost every night ever since Luna cursed me."

"I think it's safe to assume that you're looking for a person," Mrs. Scott said. "But we don't know where they are. They could be anywhere in the world, right?"

Syrena nodded.

"What about a party?"

Syrena looked at the crowd as they turned and looked to a young man with a bowl cut.

"What did you say, Gerald?" Mrs. Scott called.

"A party. It seems like Luna wants to give you a chance, otherwise why give you the five-years? And I think the signs might very well be here in town. There's no way you'd be able to find them if they weren't with you having to come back to the manor every night. So instead of you leaving the manor, why don't we throw a party and bring everyone here?"

Syrena and Mrs. Scott shared a look. A smile crept on the older woman's face. Syrena grew her own to match.

"Gerald," she said as she turned and looked at him again. "That's a great idea! Let's have a party."

The manor was abuzz with activity. The staff and plenty of help ran about, getting the place all fixed up. Decorators and planners barked commands, musicians rehearsed, and artists were busy drawing and painting away. Syrena's favorite colors were strewn about in streamers, confetti, banners, and more signs than she ever thought possible. Whenever she made an appearance to check on things, she was mobbed by people with various accents wanting her opinion. "What do you think of this?" and "Can ye taste this?" and "Should we put this over here?" and "Is this music to yer liking." It drove her insane, so she made sure she was scarce when the staff and help were most busy.

She watched the activity from the window of her room in the manor. She never knew so much went into having a party. Then again, she had never attended or thrown one before. She told herself that if and when she broke the curse, she would throw a party that would put this one to shame.

"It's quite the spectacle, isn't it?"

Syrena turned to see Mrs. Scott smiling at her from her doorway. In the daylight it was easier to make out her face and hair. Her straight silver hair was cut short, her bangs always hooked behind her right ear. Thin lips red with lipstick gave her a warm, tight-lipped smile. She wore a plain dress with a neutral color that hid dirt well. Her thick Scottish accent always brought a warmth to Syrena's heart.

"I never knew so much went into throwin' a party," Syrena admitted.

"It's much more cumbersome to throw a party than to attend one," Mrs. Scott said as she entered. "Much more fun to attend as well. Ye don't hafta clean up."

Syrena smiled as she looked down at the activity again. "I wouldn't know."

Mrs. Scott's warm hand touched Syrena's shoulder. "You will soon."

Syrena sighed. "I hope this works."

"It will, lass."

The tears suddenly came, and she looked back to her friend. "But I don't even know what I'm looking for. Just a dream that I have over and over...I could be just wasting my time...wasting *everybody's* time!"

Mrs. Scott's eyebrows lifted. "Do ye want me to cancel the party?"

Syrena sniffled. "No."

"Aye, then it will not be a waste. Ye came up with this idea for a reason, Lady Syrena. And ye don't want to cancel it because you have a feeling it will work. Am I right?"

Syrena swallowed. She *was* right. Syrena continued to have dreams about the mystery man, continued hearing his voice yet waking when she reached out to touch him. She felt that he was calling her to him, and everything Gerald had said made sense. Perhaps she had mistaken Luna afterall.

Syrena smiled and leaned into Mrs. Scott's embrace.

"Frankie and you are the worst," Syrena said.

"What makes ye say that?"

"B'cause you won't stop callin' me, Lady. For God sakes, Mrs. Scott, ye've known me since I was a little girl."

Mrs. Scott embraced her. "When ye stops callin' me 'missus', I'll stop callin' ye 'Lady.'"

Syrena looked up at her. "I'll never stop."

"And ye better not, or I'll slap yer bottom like I did when you were a lass! Now c'mon." Mrs. Scott let Syrena go and headed for the wardrobe. "Let's pick out the perfect dress fer tha party."

The entire town had been invited, and seemingly accepted. More people than she thought could fit flooded into the manor grounds. The staff were constantly hustling, offering various foods and drinks. Of course, the top requests for drink were Guinness or Irish whiskey. The noise of the party prep was nothing compared to the loud crowd that now occupied her manor.

Syrena stood at the entrance to the garden, welcoming the guests as they continued to arrive. They all offered their thanks for being invited to the party, and some expressed condolences about her father. While the Irish national colors did not overtake the crowd, there was plenty of Celtic green and bright orange to be seen. Syrena had settled on a white dress that seemed to glisten when light touched it. A way to make her stand out, Mrs. Scott had said.

She turned when a couple of rowdy men let out a laugh. They seemed to be enjoying themselves and weren't causing any trouble. Yet.

When she turned back, her eyes locked on a handsome young man coming her way. Unruly blonde hair fell over his eyes, yet there was no doubt that he was looking at her. His gray eyes instantly captivated her. The light gleamed on something on his ear, making it hard for her to see it clearly. He smiled with friendly features, and she couldn't help but smile back at him.

With a tilt of the head, he spoke. "You must be Lady Syrena."

She had to remember to breathe and nodded. "Oh, uh, yes. Thank you for coming tonight. Welcome to my home."

The young man took her hand and kissed the back of it. His lips were soft against her skin, and she felt her face heat up. At this point many men had kissed the back of her hand. Why was this one so much different?

"It is my pleasure, princess," the man said. "I don't think we've formally met. I'm Hunter Monroe."

She chuckled. "You already know my name, so it's not really fair."

His smile never left his face, and he laughed. "Indeed."

Music suddenly started to play loud from within the crowd behind them. Hunter's gray eyes looked past her and then returned. It was a happy jig; one she'd heard them rehearse to perfection a few weeks earlier.

A sly look overtook Hunter's handsome features. "Care to dance?"

She smiled and nodded, only then had she realized he had never released her hand. As Hunter guided her to a space where they could dance, she got a look at his clothes. He'd chosen black dress slacks and a light blue button up top. It did more to bring out his eyes somehow. His black leather shoes were polished and clean. She could feel everyone looking at them, and her heart quickened in her chest.

"That dress looks beautiful on you," Hunter said as they began dancing.

It wasn't her typical wear, but Mrs. Scott insisted that she wear one for her party. "Thank you. Please, call me Syrena. No one else will."

That brought out another laugh from Hunter. "Then I'll be the first. It's a beautiful name."

She searched his eyes. His smile seemed so genuine. "Thank you."

The skin between Hunter's thick brow creased. "You don't believe me?"

"I..." She opened her mouth to speak and then had to search for the words. "I've heard a lot of things lately. Some true, some...not so much."

He pressed his lips together and released her hand, placing it on her other hip and pulling her close. She thought he was going to kiss her and her heartbeat quickened, but then he moved and her head easily rested on his chest.

"You've been through quite a lot in the last few years, I know."

This time it was Syrena's brow that tightened. "You know?"

"Aye." She felt him nod even though she couldn't see his face.

Her eyes locked on the thing that had gleamed in the light. There, decorating his left ear, was a silver moon and a star, some kind of gemstone in the middle. Though it was small, the intricate design of the earring was fantastic. She found herself looking over every curve and point of the stud earring.

Hunter spoke to her with a low voice. "Princess, I need your help with something."

She looked over at her smooth jawline. "Okay. What is it?"

"Do you believe in signs? Like, from the universe?"

Her breath caught in her throat, and she gently pushed herself off him to look in his eyes. They seemed quizzical, but she didn't see any ill intent.

"It depends," she said.

Hunter looked a bit embarrassed. "Well, I have a problem. There's this traveler who I found on the street. He's from out of town, the States he said, but he says he's looking for someone. Someone important. I don't know that many important people, but I figured you would. Maybe I can bring him by and you can help him?"

Syrena chuckled. "I don't know as many people as you'd think. I've been in this manor practically my entire life. I only went out when my father needed to visit the town."

"Don't you have a library or something in your manor? The town hall didn't have many records of the people he was looking for."

"What kind of people is he looking for?"

Hunter shrugged. "He said something about a...keeper of white light."

Syrena gasped. Hunter's features jumped in surprise at her reaction.

"What?" he asked. "Did I say something wrong?"

"Are you sure that's what he said? That he's looking for a keeper of white light?"

Hunter searched her eyes and then nodded. "Yeah. It was so strange I don't think I could forget it. Do you know what that is?"

"Yes."

The song came to an end, and the onlookers began clapping for the two of them. Syrena looked to the people and gave them a smile before returning her eyes to Hunter's.

"Is he here?" she asked.

Hunter shook his head. "No, but I can introduce you tomorrow."

Syrena nodded. "Meet me at the east fountain here tomorrow at one."

"Is everything alright?"

Syrena smiled. "Actually, for the first time in a long time, something went right."

Chapter 3

To say she was anxious to see Hunter again was an understatement. All day long she took glances at the large grandfather clock in the main hall of the manor whenever the opportunity was given. Time seemed to pass so slowly. She'd replayed everything Hunter said in her head over and over to make sure she wasn't just being crazy. He'd said his companion has been looking for the Keeper of the White Light...right? Syrena shook her head at herself. What else *could* he have meant?

She ended up in the garden as the day shifted to noon. A breeze made the plants sway as she sat thinking about the events of the previous day for what felt like the hundredth time. The party had been relatively uninteresting after her dance with Hunter. The very reason she threw the party was revealed not even an hour in. She told herself she owed Gerald for the suggestion.

The key ceremony was mostly a formality since there was no other living relative to have access to the manor. It was an old Irish tradition to give a woman a key to their home when they reached age 21. She couldn't leave for long anyway, so what good was having a key? And while the food was delicious, it wasn't anything she didn't receive every day, but the townspeople seemed to marvel at the grand spectacle of the party. She supposed in the bigger picture, it was great for the townsfolk to see her happy and well taken care of.

But her conversation with Hunter had captivated her mind. So much so that Mrs. Scott had to remind her to eat and sleep, though understood Syrena's impatience with time.

When the time finally came, she quickly made her way across the garden toward the east fountain. As she neared the fountain, she saw two figures standing with their backs to her.

One was easily identified as Hunter, though his clothes were much less formal than those he had worn the previous night. His build was the same, even more pronounced from behind.

The other figure looked much leaner in frame, and his hair was a dark brown color, almost black. His clothes were definitely black, and she could tell from the look that they were not of this country.

When they heard her approach, they turned. Syrena's eyes took in the newcomer. He looked much closer to her age than Hunter's, who looked just a bit older. Still, his features were friendly, and she didn't feel threatened by his appearance. A white bandana held his hair away from his eyes. His plain black t-shirt accompanied his washed jeans that were ripped at the knees. Tattoos decorated his lightly tanned arms, and most of his fingers had a silver ring on them.

His brown eyes looked hopeful as he stepped forward.

"Are you Lady Syrena?" he asked in a friendly voice.

"I am," Syrena replied.

"I'm Austyn Martin," the young man answered. "I came from 'alfway 'cross the world to meet you, princess."

Syrena blinked and had to think about what he said. It didn't sound like anyone from Ireland. She looked to Hunter, who gave her a nod.

"Where are you from?" Syrena asked.

"Jersey."

When she lifted a brow, he continued. "It's in the United States. Wait, you've never even *'eard* of Jersey?"

Syrena shook her head. "I've been trapped in this manor for most of my life. I was told you're looking for the Keeper of the White Light," she asked. "Is that true?"

Austyn got ahold of his shock and answered. "Yes."

"And who told you about this in...Jersey?"

Austyn looked away from her, looking a bit doubtful and defeated. "This is gonna sound crazy, but I promise you it's the truth. I started 'aving this dream. I...I see this queen. She's got a light in her chest...like *inside* her body." He hesitated. "I never talked to her, but I woke up with these thoughts about the Keeper of the White Light. I looked everywhere, but there's nuttin' about it in Jersey. Then, someone told me 'bout an old legend back where they were from, here in Ireland. So, I came here to check it out. I ran into Hunter here." He gestured toward Hunter. "And when I explained my dream to him, he said he wanted to help me. D'you know where I can find the Keeper?"

After deciphering what Austyn said, Syrena nodded. "You've found her...sort of."

Doubt and suspicion took over both of their features. "Sorta?" Austyn said.

Syrena sighed. "My mother was the Keeper. She was supposed to guide *me* so that I could take over once my time had come, but she died before she could. My father didn't tell me about any of it, so when the enchantress came, she didn't think I was ready for it, so she cursed me to test me. Now, I have to break this curse before my birthday next September or the White Light will fade, and the town will be taken by the darkness."

Hunter and Austyn shared a look.

"And what'll this darkness *do*?" Austyn asked. He shook his head. "I'ont recall seeing any darkness when I flew over."

"That's because it's not something you can see."

Syrena and Austyn looked at Hunter. He'd looked off and seemed to be deep in thought.

"What you said actually makes a lot of sense," His eyes returned to her, "Syrena. It answers questions to something I'd been wondering about. A lot of people have been so irritable lately. People who were always nice. I thought maybe they just had bad days or something. There's been a lot of fights in the town, too. I thought it was just bar speak, but if what you're saying is true, Syrena, then the people here are in a lot of trouble."

He looked back to Austyn and Syrena. "We *have* to break this curse and restore the White Light."

Austyn nodded in agreement. "I remember dealin' with some of the townsfolk. I thought I was back in Jersey for a second there."

"Definitely not." Syrena looked back at the manor. "I'm suddenly very hungry. Did the two of you eat lunch?"

Both men shook their heads.

"Good. Come with me. I'll have the chefs make us a meal. What do you feel like eating?"

Austyn thought a moment. "D'ya got corned beef? I've heard it's delicious. I've wanted ta try it since I got 'ere."

Syrena and Hunter stopped in their tracks and looked at him.

"You've *never* had corned beef before?" Hunter asked.

Austyn's eyes went from one person to the other as he shook his head. "I told you I'm not from 'ere."

"Don't they have it where you're from?" Syrena followed.

A patient smile spread on Austyn's lips. "If they did, I wouldn't have asked for it, now would I?"

That brought out a bellowing laugh from Hunter. "The man has a point."

"He certainly does," Syrena added. "Alright, corned beef it is, then. Follow me."

Austyn sat back in his chair with a satisfied smile. "Aaah, that was fantastic. Thank you so much, Syrena."

She gave him a smile. "My pleasure. It's probably the most famous dish in Ireland."

Hunter chuckled. "I don't know. Irish whiskey is close to becoming its own food group."

The group had a laugh. As the staff reappeared from the kitchen to clear the table, Austyn sat up and leaned his elbows on the table. His expression became more serious.

"So, let me get this straight," he said. "You can't stay out of the manor past midnight. If you do, you'll age a year, right?"

Syrena nodded. "Yes. At this point, the curse would be fulfilled, and the darkness would take the town."

Austyn was already nodding. "Sounds like Hunter and I will have to be the ones to search for the signs, then."

A soft thunder could be heard in the silence that followed. Syrena looked at the wall where the windows showed the gray clouds looming over the trees.

"That looks bad," she said.

"And it came quickly," Hunter added. "We were just out there an hour ago. I didn't see a cloud at all."

"Focus, guys," Austyn said. "You wanna break the curse, don't cha?"

"Yes, sorry," Syrena said. "You're right." She put her attention back on the young man from Jersey.

"D'ya got any information about the signs?" Austyn asked.

Syrena shook her head. "All Luna told me was that I needed to find them before my twenty-first birthday."

"Okay. Let's say you find the signs. Then what?"

"Then we stand on the Sign of Purity and break the curse."

Austyn tilted his head slightly in confusion. "The Sign of Purity?"

Syrena stood from the table. "It's easier if I show you."

She walked around the table back toward the main entrance. In the main hall, the marble floor glistened in the chandelier light that was cast down from above. The roof was a windowed dome, and the clouds grew more and more ominous above.

Seemingly painted inside the marble were black markings that curled into a thick, wide circle. At three places in the circle, were white circles big enough to fit one person inside. There were some markings drawn inside each circle in black that didn't look like any recognizable language. Lines went from each circle on toward the middle until they met at another circle. All of the smaller circles had different markings in their center.

Austyn walked out toward the symbol in the marble and inspected it.

"I didn't even notice when we walked ova it," he said. "Any idea what these symbols mean?"

Syrena shook her head with a frustrated sigh. "I wish I did. Maybe I'd know a little more about what I'm looking for. Gerald did say something that made sense, though."

Austyn looked up at her. "Who's Gerald?"

"One of the staff here. With my curse, I can't leave the manor so it makes sense that the people I'm looking for are here."

"Or *coming* here," Hunter added. "Austyn's not from here, but he found a way."

Syrena nodded. "And from what you said, Austyn, it seems that the people I'm looking for are also having strange dreams. That definitely narrows things down."

"Yeah, but how do we find the others?" Austyn asked. "We can't just keep throwin' parties every day."

As Syrena opened her mouth to speak, a loud crack of thunder sounded and the lights flickered. The sounds of heavy rain tapped on the ceiling, bringing all of their heads up.

"I certainly hope that's not a sign of what's to come," Hunter said.

"Whether or not we're on the right track, I think it's safe to say that nothing's going to happen tonight. No one is showing up with *this* kind of storm." Syrena looked to her new companions. "You guys are not walking out in that. You're welcome to stay here if you'd like."

The boys shared a look, and Austyn shrugged. "It's not like I have anyone who is waiting for me."

"Me neither," Hunter said. "Alright, Lady Syrena." His smile returned and he bowed deeply. "Looks like we're your guests for the evening."

Syrena walked past him and grumbled. "I thought we agreed that you would call me Syrena."

Hunter lay on the soft bed looking up at the grand ceiling of the manor. Painted on the white background was a picture of the Eiffel Tower complete with a grassy plain and a partly cloudy sky. Nothing like how it looks now. There was no tourism, no shops at the base of the tower. It looked peaceful and serene.

Much like he felt when he was with Syrena.

He couldn't really put his finger on it, but he felt drawn to her since the day he laid eyes on her at the manor party. Her captivating blue eyes contrasting with her raven hair made it hard to look away. The fact that she looked completely nervous that day at her party did more to make him smile than to repel him. Her ability to stand tall and make the effort was...cute. Admirable. He idly wondered why there seemed to be no man in her life. Word about the princess was aplenty in town. She had turned down guy after guy after guy. Guys who he felt would be well suited for a princess like her. Successful men, handsome men. But for whatever reason they all came back with the same defeated stories.

A knock at the door brought his attention to the wooden barrier. "Yes?"

"It's Syrena."

Hunter rolled out of the bed. "Come on in."

The door opened easily with barely a sound, and Syrena stepped through. When their eyes met, she smiled and came further into the room.

"Are these accommodating enough for you?" she asked.

"More than enough," Hunter said as he walked over to the window showing a grand view of the town, adorned by a beautiful cloudy sunset. "With views like this, I don't think I'll ever want to leave."

Syrena laughed. "I'd be okay with that. It gets lonely around her without anyone around."

Hunter looked over at her. Her eyes went to one of the grand dressers in the room. "You've got the staff."

Syrena nodded with a distant smile. "Yes, but I don't really get to talk with them much. Well, besides Mrs. Scott."

Hunter tilted his head. "Mrs. Scott?"

Syrena looked up at him. "She's been with me since I was a young girl. I can honestly say if there's anyone who knows me, it's her." Syrena's expression dropped as she looked out the window Hunter's body faced. "Anyone left, at least."

Her eyes seemed to stare off into the distance. Hunter looked out the window again, his insides aching for her. He'd heard about her losing her parents, and he thought about what he would do if he lost his. He couldn't even imagine.

"Looks like it's stopped raining," he said, trying to change the subject. "I never knew the sunsets could be so beautiful."

Syrena's footsteps were soft against the carpet as she came to stand next to him. "I've never seen it from this view."

His eyes went to the translucent reflection of her in the glass. "Where do you usually see them from?"

"The garden, or," she hesitated, "...my room."

"Hm. Is it better than this view?"

"The garden, no. My room...yes. Much better."

"Well...I envy you. But this...it could certainly be worse."

They stood watching the sunset for a while. Finally, Syrena broke the silence.

"Is that the only reason you came to the manor?"

Hunter looked over at her. "Hm?"

She peeled her eyes away from the sunset. "To ask for my help with Austyn."

"Oh." He looked back out the window and tilted his head. "I hoped that you'd be able to help. I'd been looking all over town for anything that had to do with a Keeper of the White Light, but I didn't find anything. And besides, I was...curious."

"About what?"

"About you." He looked over in time to see her look at him as well. "I'd heard so many stories about the guys you rejected. I wondered what kind of woman you must be. Some of those guys had a lot of women chasing them, but not you." He laughed. "It was good to see them put in their place for once."

"Oh." Syrena looked down. "I didn't mean to hurt their feelings."

"Why did you reject them? Didn't you think they were good looking enough?"

Syrena chuckled and looked out the window again. "There's more to relationships than looks. Yes, some of them were very good looking, but...I don't know. I guess I'm waiting for something a little more...pure."

Hunter nodded his understanding. "With what I now know about you, you definitely deserve someone special. Hopefully you find him."

Syrena breathed a sigh. "Hopefully."

"Let's break this curse first, and then...who knows? But at least you'll be free."

She smiled. "I can't wait to be free."

"After the curse is broken, would it be too much trouble if I came to visit from time to time?"

She looked over at him and blinked. "What?"

Hunter shrugged, starting to feel embarrassed that he'd asked. "I'd like to come visit sometimes if I could. I wouldn't want this friendship to be over just because you don't need my help anymore."

"Do you really mean that?"

"What? That I'd like to come visit?"

"No...that we're...friends."

He could see her chest rising and falling with her slightly rapid breathing. "You really haven't been outside the manor much, have you?"

Syrena shook her head. "Hard to make friends that way."

"Definitely. Yes, I consider us friends."

Syrena's beaming smile warmed his heart. "Then yes, you can visit from time to time."

Hunter's sly smile returned. "Can a friend see the sunset from your room?"

"I..." She closed her mouth and cleared her throat, turning from the window. "I'm going to bed. Good night, Hunter."

He watched her walk away, his smile growing. She never turned, and soon the door latched as she closed it behind her. Hunter turned back to the purple, orange and yellow sky.

"Good night, Syrena."

Syrena took a settling breath, her hand still on the doorknob as she closed the door behind her. Thoughts of the conversation caused her heartbeat to quicken and her face to heat up. Her ears even felt hot.

"Charming little devil, isn't he?"

The whisper from behind caused her to jump and whirl. Mrs. Scott stood a little ways away, giving Syrena one of the most mischievous smiles she had ever seen.

"Mrs. Scott!" she said a little louder than she expected. Her eyes went to the door and then she quickly strode away from it to her friend. "How long have you been standing there?" she whispered harshly.

Her smile seemed to grow. "I got here right around the time you told him that you wouldn't mind him staying here. Looks like you've got a crush, dear."

Syrena almost let out a laugh. "Then you must not have been listening. He said we were *friends*."

She felt Mrs. Scott's hands on her shoulders as the woman guided her down the grand hallway. With a little too much joy in that hum of hers.

"Lass" she said as if she were speaking to a child, "I know what it sounds like when two people are interested in one another. It's *okay*. You're a pretty young princess, you're *supposed* to like handsome young men like him. What's his name again? Hunter?"

She whispered his name in her ear teasingly, bringing out a squeal from Syrena. Which just made Mrs. Scott laugh more. Luckily, they were definitely out of hearing range, so at least there was no danger of him overhearing.

"W'll I don't see what the embarrassment's about," Mrs. Scott continued. "From what I've seen he's a perfect gentleman. And he's quite easy on the eyes. Ye could certainly do much worse."

"I don't want to think about this right now," Syrena protested, bringing her head back up to look at Mrs. Scott again. "He and Austyn are here to help me break the curse, that's all!"

"Mmmhmm, and then he'll be visitin' from time to time?"

Another groan came out, and Syrena's hands returned to her face.

"Well if ye ask I think the two of you look awfully cute together." Mrs. Scott patted her on the shoulder. "You certainly do have great taste. D'you know what he does for a living?"

"Please, Mrs. Scott..."

Chapter 4

Syrena's thoughts had no rhyme or reason as she ate breakfast the next day. As usual, the food was delicious. Unusually, Syrena had a hard time enjoying it. Syrena breathed a sigh and put another bite of food in her mouth, forcing her thoughts to the curse. She'd found one of the signs, and if what Luna had told her was true, there were two others. It made sense that they were all people, and that they were close by. But how was she to find them? She couldn't help but feel the pressure of time.

Her mind went to Hunter and their somewhat awkward exchange the night before. Mrs. Scott wasn't helpful at all! She talked about him all morning. To make matters worse, she was asking personal questions Syrena didn't even *want* to think about. The woman had no filter sometimes.

"Morning."

His voice jerked her out of her thoughts. Why was it that people always seemed to startle her all the time?

It was impossible to keep her face from warming as she looked up at him. He was dressed differently than yesterday, looking very handsome in the pants and shirt. She recognized the silky material that glistened in the light, and she mentally growled at Mrs. Scott.

Syrena cleared her throat and swallowed her food. "Morning. How'd you sleep?"

Hunter strode across the dining room and sat next to her at the table. "Like a baby bear nuzzled against his mum." He grinned at her. "Thank you. It's much better than the bed I have at home."

She smiled at him. "You're welcome. Are you hungry?"

She heard his stomach grumble, and he put a hand on it with an embarrassed smile. "I suppose it's spoken for itself."

She chuckled. "I'll have the staff give you a plate of food."

"Thank you." He leaned forward and placed his elbows on the table, folding his hands in front of him. "Soooo...any strange dreams last night?"

Syrena blinked as she chewed on another bite, making sure she swallowed before answering. "As a matter of fact, yes. Why do you ask?"

A smile formed on his face. "Did it have anything to do with you walking?"

She turned her head, looking at him out of the corner of her eye. "Yeeees...why?"

"D'ya happen to remember talking to anyone?"

Syrena opened her mouth to reply and then realization hit her. She dropped her head into her hands. As if it wasn't awkward enough. "Was I sleepwalking again?"

Hunter chuckled. "I don't know about *again*, but you quite literally ran into me last night."

Her head popped up. "I was *running*?"

Hunter scratched his bare chin. "W'll, I suppose not quite as literally as I stated. You bumped into me while you were sleepwalking, yes."

"Ugh...sorry. I had a dream that I was—"

"Walking with your Dad." Hunter's smile faded. "I know."

Syrena lowered her eyes and fought the emotions that threatened to overtake her. "It's been almost a year since he died, and I still have dreams about him as if he was still with me. He was the most important man in my life."

"Most fathers are," Hunter said softly.

The staff emerged from the kitchen and set a plate of food in front of him. Syrena watched him look around in confusion. Despite how the conversation had turned, it brought a smile to her face.

"They have a window and can see into the dining room, see?" She pointed over to a door Hunter hadn't seen. In the door was a small square window that offered a limited view of the kitchen. "It's so when the staff come in and out during dinner parties, they won't bump into each other."

Hunter made a sound in his throat as if he'd learned something new. Then he looked down at his plate. "Aaah, this looks delicious!"

Syrena laughed. "It is. Eat up! Have as much as you like."

She was glad for the break while he ate. She didn't like thinking about her father's passing. There were still nights where all she wanted to do was give him a hug.

Hunter was halfway through his plate when the door to the dining room burst open. Austyn came running in, wearing clothes similar to Hunter's. The look in his eyes brought both of them to their feet.

"Syrena, Hunter," he said, "come quick! There's someone at the door!"

Hurrying to keep up with Austyn, Syrena and Hunter left the dining room. At the grand front door, Austyn and the butler were standing there with a young girl who looked to be in her teens. Her dark clothes were drenched and looked miserable.

Syrena and Hunter came to a stop a short distance away and Syrena stepped forward.

"Hi," she said softly, "my name is Syrena. Are you lost?"

The girl stared at the floor.

Syrena knelt down to meet the girl's eye level. "It's okay. We're not going to hurt you. Do you need help?"

The girl sniffled and then nodded. "Yeah."

"Okay, I'd like to see if I can help. Can you tell me your name?"

"J-Jupiter."

"Lady Syrena."

She looked up at the butler, a tall man dressed in a suit. "Perhaps this is not the most comforting place for the girl. Maybe take her to the study. She can sit and have a cup of tea."

Syrena nodded and looked back to the girl. "Would you like some tea?"

Jupiter nodded, her eyes never leaving the floor.

Syrena smiled at the girl, even though she didn't look up and couldn't see it. "Great. If you come with me, I'll give you some. What kind would you like?"

Finally, the girl looked up. "Do you have peppermint?"

Syrena kept her smile. "Of course. Let's go to the study and you can tell me which one you like most."

Once seated in the study with a steaming cup of tea, Jupiter started to visibly relax. She looked at the bookcases covering every wall of the room, the grand desk with the comfortable red leather chair behind it, and the hand painted ceiling with the grand chandeliers offering adequate, warm lighting. Hunter and

Austyn took seats in one of the chairs in the grand room, at Syrena's request so as not to threaten the girl. Hunter decided to sit at the desk, leaning back in the chair with a satisfied smile on his face. Austyn and Syrena sat closer to the girl in neighboring chairs.

"How's that, Jupiter?" Syrena asked. "Feeling better?"

Jupiter moaned. "The tea is perfect. Thank you!"

Syrena gave her a big smile. "No problem."

"Why do they call you 'lady'? Are you a duchess?"

Syrena breathed a chuckle. "Sort of. I'm actually a princess. This is my manor."

Jupiter's eyes widened. "You're a princess?! Wow!"

"I am."

"I've never met a princess before." She looked at the other two men in the room. "And are you two princes?"

They both laughed, and Austyn leaned in. "No, we're her loyal servants."

Syrena gave him a look of annoyance. "They're *not* my servants." She smiled at Jupiter again. "They're my friends."

"And we're here to help," Hunter added with a nod. "Is there something you need help with?"

Jupiter's eyes went to the ground again. "My father. We were in an accident. The rain was too heavy and we ran into a tree." Her voice broke. "He told me to go find help, and when I did I heard an explosion. I went back, but...I couldn't find him anymore. He wasn't in the car, and it was all black."

The three friends looked at each other as Jupiter started to cry. Hunter and Austyn looked away, realizing with sadness what had happened. Syrena went and sat with her in the big chair and pulled her into a hug.

"I'm surprised we didn't hear the explosion," Hunter said. "If she was close enough to get here, we should have heard something."

"We probably did, just thought it was thunder," Syrena added. "Did your father tell you anything else?"

"No," Jupiter replied, her hands fiddling with something at the base of her neck.

"Where is your mom?" Syrena asked.

Jupiter swallowed. "She died when I was little. All I remember about her is this necklace that she gave me."

Jupiter fished out a gold chain from under her shirt. Hanging from it was a copper rose pendant. Though it was small, the majestic detail of the rose was unlike anything Syrena had ever seen.

"It's very beautiful," Syrena said.

"Thank you." Jupiter put it back under her shirt. "It's my favorite rose. I have dreams about it sometimes."

"The rose?"

"Yeah. I dream that I'm standing in a circle with friends and this rose is all sparkly. Then there's a bright light and I wake up. I have that dream over and over. It's my favorite. I feel like I'm using magic."

The three friends again shared a look. Hunter tilted his head toward the wall. When Syrena looked at him in confusion, he mimicked eating.

"Hey," Syrena said with a smile. "Are you hungry?"

Jupiter nodded. "A little, yeah."

"Why don't we get you some food."

Jupiter's eyes widened. "What kind?"

Syrena lifted both hands into the air. "Whatever you like. I have some of the best chefs in the town."

For seemingly the first time since she came to the manor, Jupiter smiled.

"What is it, Hunter?" Syrena asked after returning from getting Jupiter set up in the dining room.

"This *can't* be a coincidence," he said.

"I agree," Austyn added, "s'why I came and got you guys. It's too much of a coincidence to mean nuttin.'"

Hunter pointed to Austyn. "Exactly. Now, we have another person, appearing at your manor, who has a rose on a necklace and has repeating dreams about it." Hunter shook his head. "Too much of a coincidence."

"Do you think she's a sign?" Syrena asked.

"I'd bet on it."

Syrena looked at the door of the study as if she could see Jupiter through it, even though she was on another wing of the manor.

"What do you think we should do?" she asked.

"I think we should keep her here," Hunter said.

"It's not like she has anywhere else to go," Austyn added. "Her parents are both dead. She's an orphan."

"Is there any way we can know for sure that she's a sign?"

Hunter looked at Austyn, who shook his head. "The dream is a dead giveaway, princess."

Syrena nodded. "Yeah, I think you guys are right. Wow...what are the odds?"

"This is going to be easier than I thought," Hunter finally said. "We have ten months left and we've already found two signs." He smiled at her when she met his eyes. "We'll find the other three and break the curse in no time at all."

Syrena smiled back at him. "For the first time since this whole thing started, I actually think we can."

Chapter 5

The next month was anything but encouraging. Convincing Jupiter to stay with Syrena in the manor was easy enough, as well as the rest of the group, but finding the last sign wasn't as easy as they'd thought. They spent the month waiting for any coincidental happening, but nothing came. Not a single person visited or came near the manor since the party.

The next month Hunter and Austyn decided to go out and search for the signs themselves, telling Syrena to stay with Jupiter. They felt they could "cover more ground" with just the two of them. Every day, though, they came back with no leads or progress.

The time the boys spent out on the town was time Syrena had to get to know one another. She went with Jupiter to the seamstress to get her sized for new clothes. Jupiter seemed to prefer dark clothing and rejected anything not black or, strangely, the same glossy red as her hair and lips. She learned that Jupiter was from Paris and spoke French and English. During the day they'd drink tea and talk about the wonders of Ireland and France. Syrena put France on her mental list of places she wanted to visit once the curse was broken.

When she wasn't with Jupiter, Syrena went to the study and looked for any information about her mother. Unfortunately, there weren't any records in the study. Not even a diary. She did find something about the Keepers of the Light in a book of old legends, and she took it to the desk to study intently.

She was in the middle of taking notes on the history of the Keepers when Hunter came in.

"I hope I'm not interrupting anything."

Syrena looked up and saw him leaning on the door frame. His hair was a mess, which was typical, but something about it today made him look...different somehow.

She shook her head. "No, nothing I can't pause. Is everything alright?"

Hunter stepped further into the study and breathed a sigh. "Actually, no. We're not making as much progress as we'd hoped. We've no more information than we did a month ago.

Syrena nodded and pressed her lips together. "Okay, any ideas on what to do next? We still have quite a bit of time."

"Austyn thought up an idea that I think might work. He says we should ask anyone if they've had any strange, recurring dreams. Maybe that will help narrow the focus."

Syrena lit up. "That sounds like a good idea! Maybe the staff will have some others in case that doesn't work. I'll talk to Mrs. Scott when I have a chance."

Hunter nodded. "Excellent. What are you reading?"

Syrena picked up the book so he could see the cover. "The Keeper of the Light. I found it here when I was looking for more information on my mother. It's a very interesting read." She put the book down and turned back to the beginning of the book. "It says here that the Keepers were the protectors of an ancient magic that kept the people from the Keepers of the Dark. Apparently, there were two sides constantly fighting to take the people back then."

"Really?"

"Mmhmm." Syrena nodded at him and scanned the book for the place. "Back then the people were susceptible to temptation by what they called the Dark Gods. They said they saw shadows with purple eyes telling them to do bad things."

Hunter came around the desk to look over her shoulder. "This is starting to feel like we're in *The Avengers* or something."

"It *does* feel like this is more important than I thought. My question is why is the darkness targeting *this* town when there's a Keeper here."

Hunter made a sound in his throat. "That's a good question. It does seem like a lot of effort for a small town. There must be some other reason."

Syrena turned the book back to the page she was working on. "Jeet?"

Hunter looked at her confused, and then he laughed when he realized what she'd said. "You're turning into Austyn now?"

"Just trying out his Jersey slang. He's been teaching me a bit of it. I think it's a much easier way to get the message across sometimes."

"Well, I would rather only hear it from him. I have to deal with him every day, and sometimes I want to hear regular English."

Syrena laughed as she stood. "Understandable. You have to admit, Jersey's an interesting place."

"It's probably at the top of your places to visit, right?"

Syrena walked with Hunter around the desk. "Actually, I think Paris is. Jupiter's been telling me about her home, and it sounds marvelous."

"*Any* place sounds marvelous after you've been cooped up in a manor all your life." Hunter laughed. "The world is wonderous.

I've been to Paris a few times. I'll take you there once this curse is broken."

Syrena smiled as they left the study. "I'd like that. I'll need a guide."

Things didn't pick up with Austyn's idea either. What looked like a positive response at first turned into "a bunch of bull", as Austyn would say repeatedly. They received written documents of every weird dream the entire town had, from flying high above the town to falling through the ground and talking with the magma monster that was the core of the earth. Not one of them were close to the dreams Austyn and Jupiter had. Every day they came back with disappointment etched on their faces. Syrena did her best to keep things happy when they returned home, but even she admitted to herself that things were looking more and more hopeless as the next month passed. Austyn in particular grew more and more agitated as the days passed.

During December, Syrena refused to allow the negative thoughts to darken the holiday season. She stopped all searching for the signs and had the entire manor decorated in gold with a huge Christmas tree put up in the grand hall where the symbol of Purity was. They all went into town during the day to buy gifts for each other with money Syrena took out of the family account, and Mrs. Scott volunteered to secretly gift wrap each present.

For dinner, a grand feast was made, and Syrena had everyone, staff included, indulge in the dining room. The manor was full of talk, laughter, and life for the first time in a long time.

As she sat back in her chair, Hunter, seated next to her, raised a question.

"Just how are you able to afford all of this?"

She looked over at him, puzzled. With his chicken leg, he motioned toward the sky, indicating the entire manor. Syrena looked at the walls as if the story was written on them.

"From what my father told me, the town gives our family money. I didn't understand why then, but now I feel like it has something to do with the White Light."

Hunter looked around the table at the staff, but Syrena shrugged away his concern.

"They all know about the curse. How do you think we came up with the party idea?"

Hunter gave an understanding nod. "Seems you have more help than I thought."

"Yeah, but I need the staff here to take care of the manor. They give me ideas when they have them, but mostly they focus on their duties here. I need all the help I can get."

"We're not going anywhere until this curse is broken," Hunter said with a smile.

Syrena scowled at him. "No curse talk. It's Christmas!"

With that, Syrena raised a glass to the table. "Merry Christmas all!"

They returned the gesture, and the talk went back to being joyous.

After dinner, presents were shared before everyone retired for the night. Jupiter, Hunter, and Syrena sat in front of the grand fireplace in the family room with steaming cups of tea. Austyn decided to go to bed early as he "wasn't a big tea fan".

"I don't understand how you don't drink tea?" Jupiter said.

Syrena laughed. "He's not from Europe, Jupiter. Where he's from, they drink coffee."

"We drink coffee, too. *And* tea."

"Coffee is more of a morning ritual for the Americans," Hunter said.

Syrena looked over at him. "Have you been there?"

Hunter took a sip of his tea and nodded. "Yeah, lots of times. The way they drink coffee is different than the European way. They have coffee shops on practically every corner. They do more to sweeten it than we do, though. By the time they get to drinking it, it's more like sweetened milk than anything else."

"You don't know what you're talking about."

Everyone turned to see Austyn walking into the family room. "That's how the women and the pretty boys drink their coffee."

"Austyn!" Syrena stood up to greet him. "I thought you weren't a tea fan."

"I'm not," he replied. "I just wanted to hang out witchu guys." He grabbed one of the sitting chairs and placed it next to the group's. "And by the way, you guys have lattes and stuff out here, too. I'm pretty sure 'latte' isn't an American word."

Syrena looked over at Hunter with a laugh. "He's got a point."

"As for me, I drink my coffee with just a little milk, no sugar," Austyn explained. "Gives me a little boost, ya know?"

"You haven't asked for coffee here once," Syrena said. "We have coffee here."

"I was told that European coffee isn't as strong as American coffee."

Hunter laughed. "What idiot told you *that*?!"

"A friend o' mine."

"They obviously haven't been here." Hunter chuckled. "European coffee is definitely stronger than American, overall."

Austyn looked at the group and nodded. "Alright then, I'll have some tomorrow. You got milk out here?"

The group laughed at his sarcasm.

"All joking aside," Austyn started, "I think we should talk about our plans moving forward. This little break is good and all, but we still got a curse to break."

Hunter sighed. "I have to agree with him. I've been feeling like I should be doing something more to help break the curse."

"Me too," Jupiter said.

Syrena took another sip of her tea with a nod. "I understand. My mother told me that when it seems like you're not making progress, take a break and get away from it for a bit. That's all I was trying to do."

"And we appreciate it, princess, honestly," Austyn added. "It was better than any Christmas I've had with my family, lemme tell you."

Jupiter blinked. "Do you celebrate Christmas differently in the U.S.?"

Austyn shook his head. "Nah, there's just a little more alcohol involved. Then people get a little too bold. And I have a big family with a lotta unresolved issues. They like to tell each other about it when we get together every year."

"Sounds awful," Syrena said.

"It is," Austyn chuckled. "'Specially when there's alcohol involved. But this...this was nice."

"I agree," Hunter said, "one of the better Christmases I've ever had."

"It was my first Christmas alone."

Everyone turned to Jupiter, who was staring at the fire.

"But I never felt alone because of you," she continued, looking over at Syrena. "I thought it would be harder, but this was one of the best." She smiled. "Thank you."

Syrena had to swallow to keep the tears from coming. Her nose stung as emotions boiled over. "You're welcome. I wanted all of you to know how much I appreciate your help. I didn't want this to be about the curse and nothing else."

"We know," Austyn said. "But if you don't mind, I'd like to get back to work tomorrow and figure out how we're going to break this curse. I got some ideas, but we can talk about that later. Maybe over a cup of your European coffee at breakfast."

The group laughed.

"Fine," Syrena said with a nod. "Tomorrow at breakfast, we get back to it. For tonight, how about we just enjoy this fire and you all tell me where I should visit first once this curse is broken. Jupiter's been telling me a lot about Paris."

Austyn scoffed. "Paris ain't got nothin' on Jersey. I'll tell you why..."

Chapter 6

"**I** don't know how to find the last sign."

Syrena looked up from the book of the Keepers to see Austyn standing in the doorframe looking defeated.

"We tried everything, princess," he continued as he walked into the study. "I even stood on rooftops to see how the townsfolk were walking around. Looking for someone who looked lost, ya know? I got nothin.'"

Syrena sat back in her chair. There was only a month left and since they'd found Jupiter, they hadn't even found a clue as to where the next sign could be. Anxiety had started to build up in her chest as the season turned to spring and rose once summer hit. She started thinking about her past actions and how she could have done things differently. Maybe she shouldn't have insisted everyone take Christmas off. Looking back on it, breaking the curse would ensure *more* Christmases in the future. She wished she would have thought of that. Maybe she should have been searching outside the manor herself to help.

But if Austyn and Hunter couldn't find any clue as to where the next sign would be, what would her joining the search accomplish? And what if something happened and she was out past midnight? Then it all would have been for nothing. There had to be something else. Something they weren't seeing or had overlooked.

Syrena looked back at him. "What *do* you know?"

Austyn pressed his lips together in frustration. "As soon as we started looking, seems like everything dried up. Suddenly no one had even *heard* of the old legend. I came from the US and I heard it out there. Either someone's lying, or there's something else going on 'ere."

Syrena looked off again. "Or maybe we've been going about this the wrong way."

"What do you mean?"

Her eyes flashed back to him. "You said it yourself. As soon as *we* started looking, everything dried up. Before, the signs seemed to come to me. Once we went to search, we started failing."

Austyn made a sound in his throat as he contemplated what she said. "So, you're thinking we gotta wait for the sign to come to us again?"

Syrena leaned forward. "Perhaps it's a bit out of the blue, but I was thinking about this the other day. Any time someone talks about signs, what do they say?"

Austyn shrugged. "Depends on the kind of sign, I guess."

"I mean spiritually...or *whatever*, really. You always *wait* for a sign, or the signs come to you."

Austyn's jaw opened as he aligned with her thinking. "You know what you got a point there. Even when you're driving, you don't go lookin' for signs. They're there already."

"W'll I've never driven, but I see your point. No one has ever said 'I'm going to look for a sign'. Maybe this is the same thing."

Austyn gave her a resigned expression and he shrugged. "I'm willing to try anything at this point. I sure hope you're right, princess. There's only a month left before the curse is permanent."

Syrena nodded. "I know. I just can't help but think I'm right. I mean, you found your way here all the way from Jersey. I don't think that's a coincidence."

There was a sudden flash of light in the room, causing both of them to recoil. When she recovered, Syrena saw Luna standing beside her desk. Her golden hair seemed to flow out behind her, even though she stood still and there was no wind. She wore a majestic white dress with golden frills around the neck and wrists.

"Syrena." Her voice seemed to echo in the room.

"Luna," Syrena answered as she stood from the desk.

"You are running out of time."

"Thanks Captain Obvious," Austyn said, looking at Luna with annoyance.

"Austyn..." Syrena softly reprimanded before turning her attention back to Luna. "Pardon my friend. He's been helping me look for the last sign and is just frustrated."

Luna's brow lifted as her eyes glided to Austyn. His hard gaze never faltered. Neither did Luna's.

"I need more help, Luna," Syrena continued. "We need to know how to at least *know* who the last sign *could* be. Are the signs in the same situation that I am?"

Luna's face returned to its emotionless mask as she refocused her attention on Syrena. "What do you mean?"

"Are they told about their purpose by their family members? If the members die or aren't there, they'll never know."

Luna gave her a small smile. "Very astute, Syrena. Yes. The signs are beings of magic that are passed down through trusted generations."

Syrena nodded. "That's what I thought."

"Who are you?! Another princess?"

Everyone turned as Jupiter and Hunter entered the room, Jupiter's eyes wide as she looked at Luna. Luna's expression never changed.

"I am Luna," she said. "I am not a princess; I am a Keeper."

"A keeper of what?" Jupiter asked.

Syrena beckoned Jupiter over with a hand, which Jupiter took when she was close enough.

"Luna's a Keeper," Syrena said. "She's the one who put the curse on me."

Jupiter's entire aura changed as she looked back at Luna with fire. "How could you do that to her?! She didn't do anything to deserve that!"

"It was necessary," Luna said calmly. "I don't expect you to understand."

"You got a problem with kids or somethin'?" Austyn said.

"Guys, please!" Syrena exclaimed. "This isn't going to help us solve the problem so let me handle this." She looked at each of them to make sure they wouldn't add anything more. They all obliged but weren't happy about it.

Syrena looked back to Luna. "Luna, we need help. My time is running out, and then the darkness will have the town. When I was a child, you told me once that we were on the same side. Will you help us find where the next sign is?"

Luna watched Syrena in a way that made her heart rate quicken. "Very cleverly put, Syrena. I am sorry, but this curse is your burden to bear. I cannot help you."

And for the first time ever, Luna looked sad as she continued. "Any assistance from me will make the curse permanent, and then the darkness will have the town and more. I do understand the burden you bear, but I cannot interfere."

"Her not telling you is her only way to help you," Austyn said, more in realization to himself than to everyone else.

"That's right," Luna said, her voice matching her expression. "I cannot break the rules of the Test of Purity. You must find the signs in your own way."

Syrena took a settling breath and nodded as she looked at the floor.

"Your frustration is understandable, Syrena," Luna continued, "but you must not let it darken your heart." Syrena heard Luna approaching but was too ashamed to look up. "If you were not *able* to break the curse, you would not have made it this far."

Syrena's face warmed as Luna's hand reached out. With two fingers, Luna gently lifted Syrena's chin so she could look Luna in the eyes.

"Believe in yourself," Luna said, her face a picture of cool confidence, "and trust those whom you have befriended." She shook her head slowly. "You do not need my help."

Tears flooded Syrena's eyes and fell down her cheeks. She sniffled and nodded against Luna's fingers. Only then did Luna let her hand drop, the warmth from her light leaving Syrena's face feeling cooler.

Luna's eyes went to the group. "When you are feeling discouraged, seek comfort in each other." Her eyes returned to Syrena. "Believe in yourselves. Together you are strong."

Syrena, now regaining her composure, nodded and stood taller. "I will break the curse."

Luna offered a small smile to her and the group before she disappeared in another flash of light, leaving the three of them staring at where she had been.

"I don't like her," Jupiter said bitterly.

"I'm not a fan either," Austyn added.

"Are you alright, Syrena," Hunter asked softly as he came to her side.

Syrena chuckled as she continued to stare at the place where Luna just stood. "I will be."

"I suppose Austyn filled you in?"

She nodded. "Yeah, and I actually have another theory on why we're having trouble, but..." She looked around the study. "Right now, I just want to get away from all this."

The group was silent for a moment before Austyn perked up.

"Hey, you know what? Back in Jersey when I was upset, I'd walk downtown and it always made me feel better." He pointed over his shoulder with a thumb. "I found some trails in the forest I can take us to."

Syrena considered his idea and looked to Hunter. He lifted his brows and tilted his head, implying that he wasn't against the idea.

"Alright," Syrena said, "but let me go change first. These morning clothes aren't for walking. And remember, we can't stay out for too long."

Hunter laughed. "If we're walking from now until after midnight, we *definitely* have bigger problems."

Austyn's idea turned out to be just what Syrena needed. She was already fond of nature and spent most of her time in the garden, but the liberating feeling of being away from the manor gave her an excitement she wasn't expecting. She practically skipped down the trail Austyn led them to, and the four of them spent the walk talking and joking among themselves. For the moment, the curse was a distant memory.

Austyn entertained them with stories of how people talked back in Jersey, and they spent a few laughing moments mimicking the Jersey accent and slang. One such moment had Austyn and Jupiter walking ahead of Syrena and Hunter, creating scenarios where they ordered ice cream with "jimmies" rather than sprinkles.

Hunter breathed a chuckle as he watched and listened to them. "Jersey sounds like a strange place."

Syrena smiled, also entertained by the duo. "I'd like to visit it. Anything is better than looking at the manor walls twenty-four-seven."

"Oh yeah," Hunter laughed. "I guess that's a different perspective."

"What about you?" Syrena asked, looking over at him as they went. "What brought you to Tara? Seems a slow place for a guy like you."

Hunter sighed as he looked off. "I got tired of the big city life. Sussex is beautiful, but it's just not for me. Too many people, too many tourists." He looked back at her. "I enjoy the simple life with a small group of friends."

Syrena scoffed. "I'd be happy to switch positions with you. Once we break this curse, I'm traveling everywhere every chance I get."

"Traveling to a place and living there are two different things," Hunter said. "I'd be happy to travel everywhere. You can experience the great things and leave the craziness behind as you head to the next place."

Syrena let out a little moan. "Sounds amazing."

"Your parents never took you anywhere before you were cursed?"

Syrena shook her head. "Mother died when I was very little, and father just got worse and worse as the years passed. *Now* I know why. Before, I thought it was just because of Mother."

Hunter nodded before she finished her sentence. "Aye, that's a hard thing to deal with. I don't like talking about my mother, I can't imagine if my wife had passed."

Syrena's head snapped over and stopped walking. "You have a *wife*?!"

Austyn and Jupiter looked back at Syrena's outburst.

Hunter looked at her as if she was stupid. "You think I could be away from home as long as I have been if I did?"

Syrena's face warmed. It was a valid point.

"I meant if I was married," Hunter clarified, "I couldn't imagine the kind of person I'd be if I lost her."

"Oh." Syrena started walking again, feeling more than a little embarrassed. "I'm sorry."

"Why so concerned?" The way he said it brought her eyes to his again, and the sly smile he had filled her with dread.

Syrena stammered. "I-I...just wanted to make sure you were taking care of your responsibilities. That's all." She couldn't help the heat that hit her face and ears.

"Well," Hunter's slyness left his voice, and he looked ahead again as Austyn and Jupiter resumed their Jersey talk, "one day, when I have one, I will."

Syrena smiled in spite of herself. "I think you'll be an excellent family man."

When their eyes met again, Hunter gave her a different kind of smile. A smile that warmed her from the core. She had to focus to steady her breathing and looked away from him with great effort.

Sounds of wheels hitting pavement filled their ears. Syrena tilted her head, straining to hear the sound. As they continued, more sounds came, sounds she'd never heard before.

"Is that what I think it is?" Hunter called, quickening his walk to a run.

"Yep!" Austyn said, running ahead of him as well.

Syrena stopped, looking at the two men running ahead in confusion. "What?"

They didn't answer and instead kept running up the trail. Syrena looked toward where the sound was coming from but saw nothing but trees.

"What is it?" she said louder.

"C'mon Syrena!" called Austyn.

"Hey, hold on! Where are we going?!"

Chapter 7

The protection of the trees opened up to a big skate park. Syrena marveled at the size and popularity of it. The number of boys and girls there was a bit overwhelming for Syrena, though she didn't quite understand why. She'd just had many more people at the party at her manor. All of them seemed to have baggy clothes and flat-bottomed shoes. Some wore beanies on their heads, some had rings in their noses and colorful gouges in their ears. She found it all fascinatingly unique.

But what was more interesting was what they were doing. Under their feet was some sort of flat board with four wheels on it, two under either end of the board. The kids were using the boards to move up and down massive geometric structures, some built atop and some carved in bowl-like valleys into the pavement itself. She had never seen anything like it.

"It's called a skate park," Austyn said, seeing her awe at the spectacle.

She looked over at him. "A skate park? But no one is skating."

He laughed and took her by the arm, walking her deeper into it. "Those things the people are standing on are called skateboards. I used to have one in Jersey. When you stand on it as it's going, it's called staking."

"Oh." Syrena looked at a boy who was much younger than she as he came up the bowl and stood on the end of the board to stop his momentum. He coolly stepped on the flat pavement above the bowl and grabbed his board before turning to go back down again. "Is this the only place you...skate?"

Austyn shook his head. "Oh no. You can skate almost everywhere as long as the police allow you to."

She looked over at him. "The police?"

Austyn blinked at her. "Yeah. Don't you have cops out here?"

She stared at him harder. "Cops?"

"They call them the Guards out here," Hunter said, eavesdropping on their conversation.

Austyn and Syrena looked to Hunter, who they hadn't noticed was standing nearby. He looked over with a small smile. "Officially the An Garda Síonchána."

Austyn's brows rose. "Really?" He chuckled. "Sounds like you found that out on a Reddit board or something?"

"And had a couple of talks with old men." Hunter looked back at the kids skateboarding. "It's been a while since I've skated."

"I miss it," Austyn said, his attention also back on the skaters.

As the group watched the kids in the park, staying back enough to not get in the way, Syrena noticed a boy looking about their age with dirty blonde hair. He stepped on his board and went down the bowl, coming up on the other side. Then, when he came up again, his board slipped from underneath his feet. He flailed, almost looking like he was running in the air, and came down hard onto the pavement.

There was an audible 'oooo', and Syrena gasped. The boy rolled around on the ground in pain. Syrena made for him quickly. When she reached him, she fell to her knees.

"Are you alright?"

Wincing, he replied, "Yeah." He went to pick himself up off the ground. "The board just got away from me."

He rolled over and started climbing to his feet. When he looked up at her, his eyes widened, and he leaned away from her with a gasp.

"It's you!"

Syrena blinked and leaned back herself. "Uuuh, *what's* me?"

"It's you! You're the girl from my dream!"

The entire skate park seemed to come to a stop as the kids heard the boy's outburst. Some grouped together to watch their exchange. Syrena looked around and then back to her friends for support.

The boy scrambled to his feet quickly. "Sorry, I just...I didn't think you were real." He looked her over as if she was something he was excited to see. "I'm Phoenix Moore, what's yours?"

"S-Syrena. I'm sorry, you had a dream about me?"

Phoenix nodded. "Yeah, I've been dreaming about you a lot."

The boys in the park started to chuckle and make comments among themselves. Realization started to creep into Syrena, and she turned to her friends with a smile.

"Guys! He's been dreaming about me! It's a sign!"

"What the hell!?" came one reply form the spectators.

"That worked?!" came another.

More comments came from the boys, some praising Phoenix. Hunter and Austin came to Syrena's side. She took one of Phoenix' hands in both of hers. Excitement started bubbling up from inside.

"We've been looking *all over* for you, Phoenix," Syrena said.

Phoenix smiled. "Really?"

"Will you come back to my manor with me?"

Phoenix looked around, obviously hearing the jeers from the boys gathered around. "Uuuh, sure I guess."

"Yeah," Hunter agreed, not pleased with the comments he was hearing from the boys. "Let's get out of here."

Phoenix grabbed his skateboard and the group headed toward the exit of the skate park. Jupiter quickly gravitated toward the newcomer and offered a hand.

"Hey, I'm Jupiter," she said with a smile.

"I'm Phoenix, but my friends call me Nix."

When he shook it, Jupiter noticed the rings he had on all of his fingers.

"Hey, that's a really cool ring!"

Phoenix looked at his right hand and smiled. "Thanks."

"Where'd you get *that* one?" she followed, pointing to his pinky ring.

Phoenix lifted his pinky ring a little higher subconsciously. The thick gold band was wider than the other rings he wore and was made up of intricate designs of suns connected by their rays. It stood out against the rest of the rings he wore.

"It's my dad's," Phoenix explained. "He left it for me after he died." He shrugged. "I wear it to remember him I guess."

"When did he die?" Jupiter asked in a softer voice.

Phoenix waved his hand in the air. "A long time ago."

Jupiter reached into her shirt and pulled out her necklace. "My mother did the same for me with this necklace."

Phoenix took in the necklace and gave her an understanding nod. "It's nice."

Jupiter gave him a small smile of appreciation. "So is your ring."

They smiled at each other for a moment, then Phoenix looked at the rest of the group.

"So, are you guys like good siblings or something?" Phoenix asked.

Syrena laughed. "No, but it certainly feels like that sometimes. We've been friends for about a year."

"More than friends, princess," Austyn said. "We *live* together."

Confusion was clear on Phoenix' face as everyone else started laughing.

"It's a little more complicated than that," Syrena explained. "Can you tell me about your dream?"

Phoenix searched her eyes, doubt crossing his features.

"Don't worry," Hunter said. "No one here is going to judge."

Phoenix looked over at Hunter for a moment and then nodded. "I have a dream about this girl." He looked up at Syrena. "You. I'm standing in a circle with these beams of light, and you're in the middle. I can't really remember everything, but I saw your face. I know it's you in my dream."

"Do you know where we are?" Syrena asked him.

Phoenix shook his head. "I mean...I know we're in a room. I just don't know exactly where."

"Is anyone else there with you?" Hunter asked.

"No one besides those beams of light and her." Phoenix looked at Syrena. "What did you say your name was? Siren?"

"Sy*rena*."

Phoenix nodded. "Sorry. I don't remember anyone else but Syrena. I *do* remember being in a big room, and there were some..." He scowled and looked off as he tried to remember, "...things on the floor."

"What kind of things?" Hunter pressed.

"I don't know." Phoenix shook his head again. "I can't remember."

"That's okay," Syrena said, giving Hunter a look before returning her gentle eyes to Phoenix. "The point is that we found each other." She pointed to Austyn. "Austyn had dreams about me, too. That's why he's here."

Phoenix looked at Austyn, who confirmed Syrena's words with a nod and a small smile.

"There's a lot going on that you need to know about," Syrena continued. "You may be more important than you think."

"What do you mean?" Phoenix asked.

"I'll explain everything at the manor."

"This is it!" Phoenix ran past Syrena when she opened the door to the manor. In the main room, he looked at the designs on the ground, walking in a small circle to observe it all. "This is where we were in my dream!"

Syrena watched Phoenix. "Are you sure?"

"Yes, yes!" He looked up at her as he pointed to the symbols on the floor. "I remember these designs. I know for a fact I was here."

"Alright," Hunter said. "So, we're all here and we're all in the right place. Now what?"

Syrena's heart started to pound. She looked from Hunter to the rest of the group. She didn't know what was supposed to happen next.

"Phoenix," she said, "do you remember anything else from your dream? Anything at all?"

He looked off in thought. "I was in a circle with the beams of light."

Syrena looked at the ground. The wide circle took up most of the floor. "Do you remember how far apart you were?"

"No, I don't. I just remember seeing us all in a circle around you."

"How many beams of light?" Hunter asked.

"Uuummm...I only remember two," Phoenix answered.

Syrena went to the middle of the circle. "Okay, you guys stand in a circle around me."

Hunter stood off to the side as the three signs stood on the lines of the circle on the floor, their bodies forming a triangle around her. When they were in position, they all looked at Syrena, who stared ahead expectantly.

Nothing happened.

They all looked at each other in confusion. Syrena huffed.

"Well, now I don't know what to—"

The room suddenly darkened as if the sun had set outside, and three beams of light shot out from the three standing around Syrena. Syrena squealed at the suddenness of it all and looked at the three around her. The light wasn't around the signs, but it was coming from something on their bodies. Austyn's wrist, no, the charm on his bracelet, gleamed in light. Jupiter's was coming from her chest, though the glow was shining through her shirt, and Phoenix's was coming from his hand. With a jolt, she realized what it was. The jewels they wore were more than just special jewels, they were charms.

The beams of light slowly widened until they surrounded the signs, and their eyes then glowed gold. A low hum started in the room, and the ground began to quake. Syrena hardly heard Hunter's voiced alarm as he stood to his feet.

From the signs' eyes, golden light shot out and hit her in the chest. It warmed her, and a gold hue took over her vision. Looking down, she realized her body had been covered in the same golden light. She suddenly felt light, like a leaf blowing in the wind, and realized with alarm that her feet were no longer on the ground. Looking at her friends, she found that they were all looking up at her as she hovered in the air. The signs looked almost sinister with their expressionless faces and golden eyes. They stared at her, not seeming to be breathing.

And then, a pain hit Syrena in her chest. She wasn't prepared for the sheer violence of it and screamed in shock and agony. A thud from within her cut off her scream, and darkness took her.

The impact of dense air knocked all of them back. Hunter was slammed into the wall behind him, and he groaned as he picked himself up off the ground. The other three were also on the ground, though they were closer to the center of the room. Syrena was the only one still up.

But she wasn't on her feet.

Her body was suspended in the air, glowing the same golden color he had seen moments before. Her eyes were closed. She didn't look alive.

Hunter got to his feet and approached. There was a pressure in his ear at each step he took. After a few moments, he couldn't bear it anymore and took a step back. The others climbed to their feet as well, looking up to see Syrena.

"Is she okay?" Phoenix asked.

"I don't know." Hunter shrugged. "She's not moving."

"We have to do *something*," Austyn said. "We can't just leave her like this."

There was another throbbing warmth in Hunter's ear, and he moved his hand to comfort it.

"Hey, your ear."

Hunter looked over at Jupiter as she approached, her eyes on his ear. "It's glowing."

He turned his head as if trying to look at it, then realized how stupid of a move that was. "What do you mean it's glowing?!"

"She's right," Austyn said, also coming closer. "Wait." He narrowed his eyes. "It's not your ear. It's your ear*ring*!"

"My earring?"

"The sun and moon earring." Jupiter looked at him. "Are you a *sign*?"

Hunter searched both of their eyes at a loss. He had never been told anything about the signs. To his knowledge, no one in his family had been a sign either. There were no charms he'd seen in his entire childhood.

"Is anyone else's charms glowing?" Austyn asked the group.

Everyone looked at their charms. They were all back to normal.

"Just yours," Phoenix replied.

"It has to mean something," Jupiter said. "You have to do *something*."

Hunter looked at Syrena and then back to Jupiter and Austyn. "Each time I step toward her, my ear hurts."

"You have to try," Austyn said. He took Hunter by the shoulders. "She needs you."

Hunter looked at Syrena again. After a moment, he nodded. The group stepped back as Hunter took another step toward her. His ear started to throb. Each step he took, the throbbing got harder. Eventually, he decided to take off his earring, and he realized that the throbbing vibration was coming from the stud itself.

Holding it in his hand, he continued on. His fist began vibrating violently with each moment. Hunter grit his teeth against the pain, but he kept going. A low hum sounded when he was but three steps from her. It rose in pitch every moment, but he kept going.

Finally, he was in front of her. She wasn't moving, didn't acknowledge that she even knew he was there. He stared at her, his thoughts going everywhere. He wasn't sure what he was supposed to do next.

And then he remembered a conversation they'd had the first night he stayed in the manor. He remembered how he felt in that moment, how her face had blushed when they spoke. And over the last few days, he realized how he'd felt about her. It had nothing to do with her being a princess. It had everything to do with the kind of person she was. How she moved, how she cared for others, how she carried herself. There was no arrogance in her. Only love and kindness for others.

And he knew what he had to do.

He took a step closer and reached out for her. The gold around her body felt warm to the touch as his arm wrapped around her waist. She was surprisingly light as he pulled her to him.

"Syrena," he said softly. She didn't respond. "I don't know if you can hear me. If you can, I want you to know that I don't want to come visit every now and again, like I said. I don't want to because I want to stay here with you. If you'll have me."

His hand with his earring in it went to one of hers. He intertwined their fingers and gently brought his lips to hers.

The warmth enveloped him as he kissed her. A breeze picked up from nowhere, making him feel warm and welcome.

And just as suddenly, it was gone. He ended their kiss and looked down at her. There was no response in her features. She still had the glow around her, and her beautiful face was emotionless. He realized in that moment that she was the most beautiful woman he'd ever seen.

And then, he felt her hand give his a gentle squeeze. Her eyelids opened slowly, and her eyes found his. A smile spread across her face, and he felt her other hand caress the side of his.

"I will have you," she said.

Hunter's heart filled with joy, and he pulled her into another kiss. Her arms wrapped around his neck as she leaned into him.

Chapter 8

"Alright, we get it already!"

Hunter and Syrena ended their kiss and looked over. The other signs were staring at them. The only one who seemed happy was Jupiter. The other boys had looks of annoyed disgust on their faces.

"It's about time!" Jupiter exclaimed. "Austyn and I were wondering when you two would just admit it."

"*You* were wondering," Austyn rebutted. "I told you it was only a matter of time."

Hunter and Syrena looked at each other. Had it really been that obvious to everyone else but them.

"So, does this mean we did it?" Phoenix asked. "You're okay? The curse is gone?"

Syrena pushed away from Hunter and stood on her feet. She looked herself over. The golden glow had faded, and she was back to normal.

"I don't feel any different," she said. She looked up at Hunter. "I don't know."

There was a sudden flash of light that scared everyone. A newcomer entered the room from nowhere. Luna.

For the first time ever, she was smiling.

"You have done well, child," she said, walking toward her, her golden, brilliant hair flowing out behind her. "The curse has been broken."

The group cheered. Hunter and Syrena stood, hand in hand, watching Luna approach.

Syrena smiled in relief. "Then the town is safe?"

"Because of you." Luna nodded. "yes."

"It wasn't just me." Syrena indicated the group with her free hand. "I had a lot of help. Even from *you*, Luna. Thank you for bringing the signs to me."

Luna stopped a short distance away, her smile fading. "I did not bring them, Syrena. Your purity and gentle heart drew the four signs to you."

"But I didn't even know there *were* four signs," Syrena said. Her hand lifted Hunter's. "I never even saw Hunter's charm."

Luna turned her head slightly, her eyes ever on Syrena. "You have always seen the world in a unique way. Your dreams guided your heart. However you were able to find them doesn't matter. What matters is that you found them. And just in time.

"You have done very well, Syrena. I apologize for putting such a burden on you, but the magic that suppresses the darkness requires one with a pure heart. Otherwise, they would be consumed by it. You have proven your heart to be pure, and it is my honor to present you with the White Light."

Luna reached both of her hands toward Syrena. From her outstretched fingers, beams of white light collected into a ball above her hands. The beams shot into the ball faster until it was about the size of Luna's head. Luna kept her hands outstretched.

"It is for you to accept," she said.

Syrena was unable to see Luna through the light. She looked over at Hunter, who smiled and gave her a nod.

Syrena let go of his hand and stepped forward. When she was close enough, she reached out and took both of Luna's hands in hers.

Syrena looked at the ball of pure white light. The magic. The magic she was destined to have. "I accept."

Another light formed around her and Luna, gently lifting them off the ground. Syrena felt a breeze lift again, but it was warmer than the one before. Her body tingled as the White Light shot a beam into her chest. There was no pain this time, and somehow Syrena knew there wouldn't be any. She smiled. It felt good. Like it had been a part of her that she never knew was missing.

When the magic was fully into Syrena, she felt the ground at her feet again, and her body returned to normal. She opened her eyes, not even remembering closing them, and was welcomed with Luna's smile. "You are free to live your life as you choose," she said. "Free to leave the manor and return as you see fit."

She let go of Syrena's hands and looked to the group around them. "Protect your princess. The four signs are called to protect the keeper of the White Light from darkness here and beyond. The princess, in return, protects her people with love and devotion. That's how it has been, and how it must always stay."

Austyn, Phoenix, and Jupiter gave their agreement to Luna. Hunter returned to Syrena's side.

"With my life, if I must," he said, giving her another warm smile.

Luna's eyes returned to Syrena and Hunter. "Take care of each other." She smiled again. "You are all stronger together. Never forget that." With that, she vanished in another white light. Austyn and Jupiter ran to Syrena to hug her. Jupiter was in tears.

"I'm so happy!" she said. "We did it, you're free!"

"Thank you," Syrena said, getting emotional herself. "For helping me."

She let the two of them go and looked to the group. "This manor is too big for just me. You're all welcome to stay."

"Even me?" Phoenix asked.

Syrena looked over at him. "Of course. You just saved the entire town. I wouldn't want you to be living on your own. Did you have a place to stay?"

Phoenix looked at the ground. "W'll no. I was just staying with a few friends. I...I'd like to stay here."

"Done." Syrena looked at Austyn and Jupiter.

"Oh, you *know* I'm down to stay here!" Jupiter said. "I haven't had tea better than this place."

"Only if I have my own room," Austyn said.

Syrena laughed. "You can choose any room you like." She looked at Hunter. "It's been too long since this manor was filled with laughter. I want to bring that back."

"You will," Hunter said. His brows lifted. "But first, I want to see the sunset. You owe me a better view than the one I've had."

Syrena blushed and smiled with a nod. "You can see them every night if you like."

"So," Austyn started, looking around at the group, "what happens now?"

Syrena looked from Austyn to Hunter and then to the rest of the group as they looked at her.

And then she smiled.

READ NEXT

THE KEEPER OF THE LIGHT SERIES
BOOK TWO
HUNTER'S QUEST

HUNTER'S QUEST

THE KEEPER OF THE LIGHT SERIES BOOK TWO

Twelve-year-old Hunter Monroe lay sleeping in his bed, body twitching restlessly at the scenes that played behind his eyes. In his dreams, he saw a girl not much older than he was with a silver heart locket resting at her chest. The locket was detailed, ornate, reflecting sunlight in every which way as the girl strolled through an elaborate garden.

Then the scene shifted to one of despair as the girl raced frantically back toward a looming manor. It was night now, a storm raging in the distance and an ominous laugh towering over her as she ran. Hunter could do nothing but watch as the girl tripped and fell, then struggled back to her feet, running faster and faster only to cover less and less distance.

He woke with a start, his heart racing, sweat plastering his mane of curly blond hair to his head, his body rearing to go, ready to help the girl get to her destination. It was several moments before he was able to calm himself, to remind himself that it was just a dream. Still, even after he laid down to go back to sleep, he had a hard time getting there. Every time he closed his eyes, he saw the girl: raven-black hair, the silver locket, dressed in gauzy white. And every time he saw her, he felt that horrible desperation, like she needed him there right then, that she was in grave danger.

The dream did not come to him again for several years, and he had not thought of it since months after he'd had it. The girl faded from his mind as dream people did. But when he was seventeen, he laid down to sleep, and the dream happened again. This time, the girl stood inside the manor house having finally reached her destination. But she was obviously distressed, this time speaking to a woman sporting a slight glow about her.

"My sixteenth birthday was last week, Luna," the black-haired girl said. "What do you mean I'm now seventeen?"

The glowing woman looked down at the young girl, as if she knew much that the

teenager didn't. "You must be inside the manor by sunset or you age one year, Syrena."

Syrena.

The name clanged through Hunter, jarring him so that he awoke, sweating in his own bed just as he had with the first dream.

Aging years in only nights? Hunter thought to himself. Never had he had such elaborate dreams. Never had his dreams connected, let alone over years. But he had known the moment he saw that hair, those sapphire eyes, that it was her, that same woman from so many years ago—a girl grown up. *Syrena.*

And maybe it was the sleep deprivation, or maybe it was something else, but he almost smiled at the word. *Syrena,* he thought again. He believed it to be his favorite.

The dreams came weekly now. Never on the same day, perhaps never for the same length, but he had them weekly. And after a time, he began to look forward to them. Whether the girl was real, he hadn't the faintest idea, but he felt that he had some sort of claim on her, some sort of . . . connection . . . to her. More than anything, he waited for those dreams just to make sure that she was okay.

The older he got, the more frequently the dreams seemed to come, until he began to have them nearly every night. With the frequency, though, came an increased understanding of what seemed to occur on her end of the story. Hunter could sense something was gravely wrong at the manor. The light that had been so vibrant in her sapphire blue eyes slowly faded over time, until shortly after her nineteenth birthday, her father passed away. Gone were Syrena's smiles and shining eyes, in place leaving grief and despair and longing for . . . something that Hunter could never quite decipher.

And then one night when Hunter was just cresting twenty-one and the girl was approaching twenty, he got a dream filled with terror.

Time's up. The words screeched through the dream at him, colored with panic and fear. A flitter of images, seemingly from Syrena's own mind, bombarded Hunter. He only caught glimpses—of five different shapes, people he'd never seen, and of a girl that looked a lot like Syrena, sitting behind a huge glass window looking out, trapped forever.

Don't miss out!

Visit the website below and you can sign up to receive emails whenever Kristen Cole publishes a new book. There's no charge and no obligation.

https://books2read.com/r/B-A-VDHRB-UWAQD

BOOKS 2 READ

Connecting independent readers to independent writers.

About the Author

Kristen Cole is a writer from a small town in Arizona. As a young girl, she dreamed of becoming two things; a teacher and an author. Now years later, she is making her dreams come true. She was a reading, writing, and daydreamer in high school who turned her dreams into reality. She went into the field of education after high school with a passion for teaching. She now splits her time between teaching 4th grade and working on her next novel. She is currently working on book two in The Keeper of the Light series. She writes sweet, fun, adventure packed stories. Her characters are clever, fearless, and searching for who they are meant to be and never apologize for being different.